A HOUSEBOUND HOLIDAY

ALSO BY ALEKSA BAXTER

MAGGIE MAY AND MISS FANCYPANTS MYSTERIES

A DEAD MAN AND DOGGIE DELIGHTS

A CRAZY CAT LADY AND CANINE CRUNCHIES

A BURIED BODY AND BARKERY BITES

A MISSING MOM AND MUTT MUNCHIES

A SABOTAGED CELEBRATION AND SALMON SNAPS

A POISONED PAST AND PUPPERMINTS

🐾🐾🐾

A FOULED-UP FOURTH

A SALACIOUS SCANDAL AND STEAK SIZZLERS

NOSY NEWFIE HOLIDAY SHORTS

HALLOWEEN AT THE BAKER VALLEY BARKERY & CAFE

A HOUSEBOUND HOLIDAY

A HOUSEBOUND HOLIDAY

A NOSY NEWFIE HOLIDAY SHORT

ALEKSA BAXTER

CHAPTER 1

When I imagined my honeymoon—and I assure you I spent far more time imagining that than the actual wedding day—I never imagined that it would involve one over-active eight-year-old, his recuperating mother, and only phone calls with my gorgeous, sexy husband.

But that's what happened.

Because not long after Matt Barnes and I, Maggie May Carver, said "I do" the world decided to go into lockdown. At least we hadn't had any travel plans that were ruined. No resort in Fiji with a tropical bungalow that was standing empty, or lovely resort in some picturesque town in New Zealand or the Swiss Alps that was sending us a "we regret to inform you" notice.

Still.

No matter how I'd spun the potential possibilities for *la luna de miel* they had all involved my husband. Which meant that the reality really sucked.

But when there's a terrible infection spreading around the world and you're married to a cop and want to be able to take care of your elderly grandpa who suddenly finds himself housebound against his will, the choices are limited.

Since Matt was being exposed to every silly yahoo who thought being told to work from home meant hop into your car and go visit Colorado like you've always wanted to do, we'd made the painful yet practical decision to have him stay in the trailer with Jack, his brother, while Jack's new wife, Trish, and her son, Sam, moved in with me at what was supposed to be Matt's and my new home.

Jack had a job doing construction so he was still out and about and Trish simply wasn't up to taking care of Sam on her own just yet.

Neither was I for that matter. I think having a kid is a lot like being a lobster in a pot of slowly boiling water. Over time parents get used to all the pains and tribulations of parenthood—that's how a mom can heft a forty-pound kid onto her hip without batting an eye and make it through the teenage years without committing homicide, but one of us uninitiated fools tries to do the same? No. Not happening.

Which is how Trish could blithely ignore the sounds of her screaming under-stimulated, over-caffeinated child while Fancy—my now four-year-old Newfoundland—and I were not doing quite so well.

As Sam ran around the living room with a toy plane in his hand making vroom-vroom and shooting sounds while screaming about taking evasive maneuvers, I clutched my fifth Coke of the day to my chest and prayed for it all to end.

I'd always thought pandemics were some sort of fast-spreading wave of annihilation, not this slow-moving torture where nothing had really changed but at the same time everything had.

A Housebound Holiday

Fancy stared at me from the corner, her big amber eyes asking me what she'd done to deserve this. At least she'd stopped barking at him every time he moved. That had been the first three days. And it had not been fun chasing a hundred-and-forty-pound dog around the house trying to get her to stop.

Now she just sullenly slunk from room to room trying but failing to stay out of his way. It didn't help that we were in a two-story house and she wasn't one for stairs so she only had so many choices of where to hide.

She would've been outside where she'd been spending seventy percent of every day, but it was raining and thundering and I'd made her come in. Fancy would've happily stayed out there while tree limbs blew down and hail rained on her head, but the last thing I needed right then was an emergency visit to the vet.

I glanced towards the couch where Trish had her feet propped up on the dining room table. She flipped through her phone, never once looking up. How? How did she not notice the chaos around her?

"Sam," I said, trying not to snap the words out too forcefully, but probably failing. Even though Sam was downright adorable with his red hair and freckles, I was seriously at my limit.

"Yeah, Maggie?" He stopped, smiling at me from ear to ear.

"Will you do me a favor?"

"Sure. What?"

"I was going to go over to my grandpa's later and see how he's doing. Do you think you could draw him something for me? Like a plane? Or Lady?" (That was the miniature horse Jack insisted on throwing into my life every chance he got, including on my wedding day.)

Sam hesitated for a moment but he'd been raised with enough manners and was smart enough to know that my request wasn't really a request. He set down the plane. "Sure. Um…"

I took the plane and put it on top of the fridge. "You better get started on it now. I'd hate for it not to be done when I go over there."

"Okay."

As he slunk off towards the room he and Trish were sharing I tried to feel bad for banishing him to his room to do something quiet, but I couldn't.

Don't get me wrong, kids are cute. In small doses and at large distances.

At a loss for what to do next, I went to the kitchen and stared at the cupboards wondering what I should pick up at the store or order in.

I'd tried looking online for advice about what to store up on in event of an emergency but all the advice was for what to do if you had no running water or electricity and perhaps were living in a gym with a hundred other displaced people with nowhere to go. Under those circumstances it seemed canned goods and pasta and lots of water were the answer.

But what do you stock up on when the grocery stores are still open? And you still have power and running water?

Each time there was a story about an outbreak at a meat processing plant I ordered more meat, so we were good there. (For like the next century.)

What else, though?

I refused to buy into the craze for homemade bread that had spread through all my corporate friends.

Suddenly my Facebook feed was full of posts about sourdough starters and pictures of rye bread. (Who *ever* eats rye bread? Seriously.) I was surprised no one had bought raw wheat and a mortar and pestle yet, but give it enough time…

And I wasn't about to start my own garden. That seemed a step too far. If the world really came down to me surviving on only the vegetables I'd grown in the backyard and the sourdough starter I nurtured on a shelf each day, well, I was okay with just calling it quits at that point.

I'd miss Matt and Fancy, but no. I was just not going to go there.

But I still needed to stock up on *something*. Nice, made-by-someone else somethings. I just didn't know what.

Which is how I'd ended up with five spare jars of peanut butter, six extra boxes of peppermint tea, forty cans of soup, three dozen packets of tuna fish, thirteen cases of Coke (that I'd actually had before things went crazy but let's not dwell on that), and enough frozen meat to last for years.

Still, though, I felt like I was missing something. Maybe it was the non-food items I was missing.

But no. I had four mega-packs of toilet paper, two mega-packs of paper towels, three dozen boxes of Kleenex, six things of dishwasher detergent, two extra deodorants, one extra toothpaste, an extra shampoo, and an extra conditioner. Oh, and of course, three extra bags of Fancy's dog food and more treats than she could probably eat in a lifetime.

And yet…

Was it enough? What was going to happen next? What might be out when I wanted it?

And what was I going to want to eat that I didn't normally? Because my consumption of bacon and ice cream was through the roof.

(Not because of any "happy news" causing food cravings (although after two weeks with Sam around that would not have been happy news, thank you very much) but just because it turns out my comfort foods in times of uncertain crisis are fatty and sweet.)

I slumped into a kitchen chair and stared at the wall. I was stumped. I'd prepared as well as I could and now…

I sighed.

Now it was just a game of whack-a-mole trying to keep those I loved safe as they constantly came up with new and creative ways to endanger their health. Especially my grandpa who had somehow decided that this was all way overblown. He'd listened to me for the first week or so, but every time I turned around he was spouting some crazy half-baked idea that was bound to end poorly.

Just the day before I'd caught him trying to leave the house so he could run to the hardware store for a couple of screws to finish some project he hadn't worked on in a decade or more. I asked him if he really thought it was worth risking his life to construct a bird cage for a bird that didn't exist, and he'd just grumbled something under his breath about not being a child and being perfectly capable of making his own decisions.

I sighed again.

It was all a mess. The resort was on hold. I couldn't

see Matt or Jamie or Greta. The only bright light was that online barkery sales were thriving.

(The year before Jamie and I had started a dog barkery and human café together that had done okay, but then the land it was on was sold and the building was torn down to create a pet resort. Good news was that the person who tore it down, Mason Maxwell, married Jamie so when the resort was finally completed, we could reopen the barkery as well as a cattery and a coffee shop where Jamie could sell her delicious cinnamon buns. In the meantime, I'd left the online store up and running, and it generated enough sales to keep me from completely losing my mind.)

(And my income if Mason and Greta decided to pull the plug on the pet resort altogether. I mean, honestly, they could only pay me to sit on the sidelines for so long, right? And who knew how long it would be until we could launch a luxury pet resort given the current situation.)

There was one other bright spot. Or so I assumed.

I couldn't stumble across a dead body when I, and most everyone else, was pretty much trapped at home 24-7. (Something that had happened a disconcerting number of times since I'd moved to the Baker Valley of Colorado. I mean, seriously, how many people can die under bizarre circumstances in a series of small mountain towns? Answer: You'd be surprised.)

I glanced out the window. The storm was finally over.

"Come on, Fancy," I called. "Let's go for a walk." She scrambled to her feet and ran for the door, staring back at me like "what's taking you so long, get me out of here."

As I put on my shoes and grabbed my bag, I called out, "Hey, Trish, we're going for a walk. Be back soon."

She grunted, still not looking up from her phone. I debated asking Sam if he wanted to tag along—I knew he'd appreciate the chance to get outside—but I just couldn't do it. I needed to get away. I needed "me" time. Desperately.

Fancy cried at me, reminding me that she too needed to get away.

I hustled towards the door, leashed her up, and we dashed outside into the welcome of a mid-spring afternoon in the Colorado mountains, everything still green and fresh and alive.

CHAPTER 2

Because I had absolutely no desire to see anyone whatsoever, I led Fancy to the trail that ran up the mountain behind my house and my grandpa's house. The town of Creek is part of the Baker Valley, a string of small mountain towns off the highway surrounded by tall mountains. My grandpa's house sits at the end of town right at the base of one of those mountains, and my new home is right next door.

With the storm gone the sky was a bright, clear blue and everything smelled clean and vegetal.

(A weird word, I know, but how else do you describe that smell of living plants that can fill the air after a good storm? So different from New York where if it rained hard enough the storm drains overflowed and…Ugh. Anyway. That life was behind me now.)

It was about five hundred feet from the base of the trail to the top of the ridgeline of the nearest mountain and that's where Fancy and I headed.

After a year of being in Creek I managed the hike without gasping and needing to stop ten times along the way. (Altitude is no joke if you're not used to it.) From the top of the ridgeline we could see the entire town laid out before us. All forty-some houses, two gas stations, one church, one funeral home, and one pioneer museum which looked like they'd been around for a hundred years, and then the county seat, police station, and library which were all modern brick and shiny glass.

The town was definitely small and full of people who were a little too into each other's business, but it was home. The place I wanted to stay for the rest of my life. It had only taken me thirty-seven years and a few missed turns along the way to figure that out.

And I had Fancy to thank for starting me down that path. No way I could make her happy and live the life I'd been living in DC.

I pulled the elastic out of my blonde ponytail and twisted my hair up into a bun to get it off my neck. I liked having long hair, I just didn't like having it in the way, which sort of defeated the purpose of long hair. But I'd tried short hair. It wasn't a good look for me. At five-eight, one-sixty, longer hair was definitely more flattering.

(Which is not any sort of judgement on anyone else's weight or hairstyle choices, I might add. If you're happy as you are, be happy, whatever appearance or body shape works for you. But I digress. As always.)

Fancy, sick of waiting for me to ponder my life and fix my hair when there was a whole wet world to explore, tugged on her leash. As she led me through the knee-high grass, I was thankful that I always wore hiking boots while walking her because she was most definitely a cross-country sort of dog. Sure, I could keep her to a nice well-manicured trail, but what's the fun in that?

A Housebound Holiday

Of course, my lenience towards where she walked meant that in the spring I had to spend about twenty minutes after each walk checking her paws, legs, and belly for grass seeds. I always knew where one was by the way she'd slowly move her paw away from my grasp when I reached for it. But it still took some time and effort to find them all.

I think my record was fifty grass seeds in one walk. That one had required a set of tweezers to get them all out. But I figured as long as she enjoyed herself and I found them all, it was all good.

While Fancy stopped to sniff a very interesting tree, I glanced towards Luke's place with its backyard devoted to piles of junk. That's the one thing I don't think Matt had given enough thought to—us living next to Luke who had an annoying habit of walking around outside in skimpy little shorts and no shirt.

He was a good-looking man, no doubt about it, and always up for a little trouble-making—which women like my friend Jamie were sometimes drawn to—but I thought he was smarmy and that the world would be a better place without him.

And it was a nightmare having him live next door. Especially with Trish living with me. She was *definitely* drawn to that sort of man like a bee to honey. I'd caught them chatting in the front yard more than once. Her reunion with Jack and their subsequent marriage had been a bit of a whirlwind and now with them separated due to the lockdown I worried it might not stick. Not with a bad influence like Jack hanging around.

I didn't dwell on it too long, though, because as I was standing there on the ridge I saw my now eighty-three-year-old grandpa come out of his house and head for his truck.

"Where's he going?"

I grabbed my phone and dialed his cellphone. He hated the thing, but I'd managed to convince him that it didn't hurt to carry one. He glanced at the display and put the phone back in his pocket before getting in his truck.

I stamped my foot. "Why you…"

I stared, open-mouthed as he started up his truck and pulled out of the driveway. Maybe he was just going over to Lesley's house. Even though they were now married, they still kept separate houses. Since they were both staying home and away from danger they often went back and forth.

But no. He navigated his way to the highway, turned right, and drove straight out of town.

I cussed up a storm at that point.

What was he doing? Didn't he know how risky it was to be out and about? Didn't he understand that this thing could *kill* him?

I dialed Matt.

"Hey, Maggie. How's my girl?"

The sound of his voice alone made me smile. He was gorgeous, he was kind, and he was mine, all mine. Even if I hadn't seen him in person in two weeks.

"I miss you."

"I miss you, too. But I'm working right now. Is something wrong?"

He'd been extra busy the last couple of weeks dealing with people who had gone downright crazy thanks to the current situation. One woman who owned a vacation home in Bakerstown that she'd fled to for safety had actually called the police and demanded that they make her favorite coffee shop reopen.

A local man in Masonville had to have a truckload of fireworks confiscated because even though there was a fire ban in place he'd been setting fireworks off every single night for a week straight.

There were so many more like them…

Honestly, I didn't know how he did it. Matt was definitely a better person than I am.

"Sorry to bother you. But my grandpa just drove towards Masonville and I don't know where he's going. Will you track him down for me?"

"Maggie…"

"What?"

"He's a grown adult. He has the right to make his own decisions."

Fancy tugged on her leash. When I shook my head at her she sat down and started lecturing me in a very high-pitched, unending crying voice. For such a large dog she can be decidedly whiney at times. I grabbed a handful of treats to quiet her down as I answered Matt.

"I don't want him to get this, Matt."

"I don't either. And I'm sure he doesn't want to get it. But he knows the risks, and if he wants to take those risks…"

"Matt," I cut him off.

"Yes?"

"Just find him, please. And find out what he's up to."

There was a long enough silence on the other end of the line that I knew he was debating whether or not to argue further with me about it. But finally he just said,

"Okay. No promises. I am at work after all. But I'll see if I can't find him and make sure he's being safe. Maybe he just went fishing or something."

Fishing with a hundred other people, none wearing masks or keeping a good social distance.

"Thank you. Love you."

"Love you, too."

I hung up and looked down to find Fancy drooling all over herself, eyes fixed on the one remaining treat in my hand. "Here you go, silly girl."

She took the treat from my hand like the dainty lady she is and we continued on along the ridgeline, her sniffing at every little bush and me worrying about how to keep my grandpa safe. And how not to kill anyone before this all ended.

CHAPTER 3

The next day I decided to drop in on my grandpa and figure out what he'd been up to.

I'd learned by then not to drop in unexpectedly. I either called to get permission before I went over or I stood at the front door and knocked until my grandpa answered. No more just walking in and going looking for him, oh no siree. Only needed that experience once, thank you very much.

I didn't want him to tell me it was a bad time so I chose to walk over and knock, dragging Fancy and the drawing I'd had Sam do along with me.

Fancy, not schooled in the finer points of human behavior, didn't understand why we had to wait at the door we used to just walk through. She made her unhappiness at the delay known by crying at me.

"Fancy, I love you. But please stop."

Fortunately, my grandpa answered the door and she did. He'd just turned eighty-three the weekend before but he looked like he was in his sixties. Mostly because he was still a trim man whose hair had faded to a light brown instead of turning gray. He was wearing his customary summer wardrobe of jeans and a short-sleeved button-up plaid shirt.

"Maggie May."

"Grandpa."

I wanted to give him a hug, but since I didn't know where he'd been…

I let Fancy off her leash. She turned her crying act on him until he led her to the kitchen and gave her some sort of treat that she immediately took out the back door. I smiled to think that a year ago my grandpa would've said that the only good dog was one that lived outside and now here he was stocking up on Fancy's treats for when she came to visit.

"To what do I owe the pleasure, Maggie May? You'll see that I'm still here. Still alive and kicking. For all the good it does me." He plomped down on the goldenrod couch and reached for the front pocket of his shirt then grimaced when he didn't find the pack of cigarettes he'd kept there for most of his life. Life-long habits die hard.

"I tried to call you yesterday," I said as I sat down across from him on the other couch, moving over when a spring poked into my thigh. I stayed on the front-edge of the couch, not wanting to get too comfortable for my interrogation. "On your cellphone. Because I saw you were heading out while I was hiking."

"Huh. You know me and those new-fangled devices. Must've had it on mute. Or left it at home or something."

"Grandpa. You looked at who it was and put the phone back without answering."

He shrugged. "I was running late. Lesley and I were supposed to meet up for lunch."

"Where? Masonville? Because I watched you drive right out of town."

He crossed his arms. "If I needed a mother, Maggie May, I'd ask for one."

"Grandpa. It is not safe out there. I don't want to lose you."

"And I don't want to spend whatever time I have left cowering inside watching bad TV."

"It's just a year."

"A *year?*" He sat forward, staring at me.

"Yeah, a year. Probably. Maybe a little longer."

"I thought it was going to last for a month. If that."

"Not when we have such an uneven response and no good way to treat this thing."

"Maggie May. I love you. But I am not going to hide here in my house for the next year. It's not going to happen."

"But…"

"But nothing. I don't even know anyone who's sick."

"That can change any day. You know how many tourists flock to the valley in the summer. Matt's already having to deal with a bunch of fools trying to find somewhere they can go skiing with all the resorts shut down. Imagine what it's going to be like on Memorial Day. Or the Fourth. All it takes is one sick person and it's going to spread like wildfire. Unless you stay home. You can't get it if you're staying away from people."

He thought about it for a long moment. "So the issue is someone bringing it in from the outside?"

"Probably, yeah. I mean, there could be one or two people here who have it already. But most likely, yeah."

He pursed his lips. "What if there weren't any tourists coming in? What if it was just us? I read an article about that town, Gunnison, that never saw a case during the flu pandemic of 1918 because they locked down and didn't let anyone in."

I shrugged. "That's pretty much what New Zealand is doing. And Australia. But how are you going to do that here? We're not an island. People have second homes here, and we've already seen at least a couple bring it in with them that way. And I don't think you can just tell the rest of the state or the country to stay away. Pretty sure that's illegal under the constitution. You'd have to lock down all of America, and that's just not going to happen."

Warming up to my subject, I added, "Even here we couldn't pull something like that off. You know the big tourist companies aren't going to go along with that. They're losing money right now and have no local interests other than the tourist revenue. Why would they agree to a lockdown that cost them profits?"

"Hm." He looked far too thoughtful for my comfort. "But if we *could* keep people away…How long would we have to stay home for then?"

I sighed. "If you really could pull it off?" I thought about it for a moment. "Ideally everyone would stay where they are for at least two more weeks. Stock up on groceries, give up walking the dog or going fishing or *anything* else, just stay home and don't go anywhere. No construction. No take-out food. Nothing. I mean really lockdown, not this half-baked version we're doing now."

I scratched behind my ear, hating how dry my skin got these days. "If you did that, by the end of the two weeks anyone who had it would likely be showing symptoms. You could keep them and anyone they were locked down with isolated until they all tested negative, but let everyone else go back to their business. Of course, that doesn't cover those who have it and show no symptoms, so better to lock everyone down for two weeks and then test them all at the end of it, but that's not gonna happen."

He smiled. "Two weeks, huh? I can do two weeks."

"But that's assuming no one else was going to come into the valley after that. And assuming no one lies about their symptoms. And that people actually comply with the lockdown. But, yeah, theoretically, if all of that fell into place we could get back to normal in two weeks or so."

"So why don't we do that everywhere?"

I laughed. "Like we could coordinate that across so many states and countries? I mean, to wipe this thing out the world would have to pause for two weeks. New Zealand can pull something like that off because they're an island that's far away from everyone else. We're not. Getting Americans to all agree to do the same thing? That's like herding cats."

"But the valley's small enough, we should be able to do it here."

I shook my head. "You'd have to find a way to keep anyone else from coming in. And even people who'd been here at the time of the lockdown, if they left and wanted to come back they'd have to agree to isolate for another two weeks. No one is going to agree to do that, Grandpa. Would you?"

Even as we were having this conversation there was a small part of my mind telling me it was not a good idea to be discussing this hypothetical scenario with my grandpa.

See, my problem is, I'd probably sit down and help a murderer figure out the perfect way to kill someone as long as it was phrased as an intellectual challenge. Because when it's not real it just seems like some fun little theoretical exercise.

But to someone else? Well, my theoretical idea of how to do something might start to sound like a good plan. And my grandpa's past didn't exactly involve living by the law.

My grandpa scratched at his chin, clearly taking this seriously. "What about food? And supplies? How would you handle that?"

I swear, I'm my own worst enemy. Because instead of changing the subject, I answered. "Well, to be really safe I'd say you'd have to stop the deliveries at the border and then have some sort of contactless handoff. Or you'd have to test the drivers every time they arrived to make sure they weren't actively infective. But even that's not ideal unless you made them leave same-day. Best bet would be to stock up before you shut down and then limit deliveries from that point forward."

He sat back, thinking, which made me very nervous.

"Grandpa. You can't be taking this conversation seriously. It won't work. This is not Colorado of the early 1900s. You can't threaten people away with a shotgun or tell them they're not welcome in your town anymore."

"But if we could pull it off, we could go back to normal?"

"Theoretically, yeah. But that's like saying if I win the lottery I'll never have to work another day in my life. Problem is, how many people do you know win the lottery? And this is even harder to accomplish than that, because it's making a bunch of very different people with very different interests cooperate on something they may not want to cooperate on."

"Hm."

"Grandpa…"

"What?"

"Please don't do anything stupid."

Speaking of, I was about to ask him about where he'd gone the day before, but then Fancy started barking her head off in the backyard and I had to go deal with that instead. I loved her, but…

It had been a hard couple of weeks and I just needed a break. One little thing that would go my way.

CHAPTER 4

I called Matt when I got home. "Can you come by, please? I know you're working, but I really need to see you."

"Maggie, you know I can't risk exposing you because it'll expose your grandpa."

"You don't have to come inside. We don't have to touch. You can just stand outside the fence and I can see you, in person, for just a moment or two. Please. We'll stay six feet apart. I just…I need to see you Matt."

"Okay. I'll be right there."

"Thank you."

I paced the front yard until he finally pulled up out front. Our new house had a white picket fence in the front yard which meant that Fancy was waiting with me, too. She didn't know what she was waiting for, which is what made it all the more special when she saw Matt's vehicle stop out front and bounded to her feet and ran for the fence.

"Hey, gorgeous," he said to me as he came around the side of his SUV. He was as sexy as ever, especially in his uniform.

I went all melty inside at the sound of his voice. "Hey."

I wanted desperately to hug him and kiss him, but I couldn't. Fancy on the other hand…

She jumped onto the fence and started making pathetic, excited crying noises until he rubbed her ears and gave her a kiss on the nose and told her what a good girl she was.

I'd never been so jealous of my dog in my life.

"She misses you," I said as Fancy finally jumped down from the fence and ran to grab her newest toy—a pink fluffy bunny rabbit that I figured was a better toy for her than real rabbits.

"I miss her, too. And you."

We both stood there looking at each other, arms crossed, trying not to close that last little bit of distance.

"I wish this was over," I said.

Life has always balanced out for me. Something good happens and then something bad happens to offset it. Or vice versa.

But did life really have to follow my happily-ever-after wedding with a frickin' never-ending pandemic?

"Me too. But I'm afraid we have a long ways to go. Of course…" He glanced towards my grandpa's house. "If the reason we're staying apart is to protect your grandpa, then I think we're wasting our time."

"You found out where he's been going?"

"I saw his truck parked outside Russell's house yesterday along with about a dozen others."

"Did you talk to him?"

"I did. And he told me he doesn't know how many years he has left and he's not going to sit around at home alone on his couch watching the clock tick."

"Doesn't he realize he's going to have a heckuva lot fewer years if he isn't careful here?"

He shrugged. "You can lead a horse to water, Maggie."

"Yeah, yeah. I know. Can't make him do what he doesn't want to."

I debated telling Matt about the hypothetical conversation I'd had with my grandpa about locking the valley down somehow, but decided not to. It was probably nothing. Plus, what could he do about it? Talk to my grandpa again? Like that was going to work. No point in adding to his stress.

I glanced towards the house. "How's Jack? He giving you any trouble?"

"Nah. Barely see him. We're both working double-shifts right now. He's trying to save up for an extension to the trailer."

"An extension? What for?"

He grinned. "I think he and Trish are hoping to give Sam a baby sister or brother when this is over."

"Oh. I didn't know that. Good for them."

I tensed, waiting for Matt to say something about us having kids, but fortunately he didn't. Not that I didn't think he'd be a great father, it was just…Kids are complicated. And wanting them can sometimes destroy what's already there. So can having them. At least, from what I'd seen of my friends.

Oh, there were the happy, delighted, bonded-by-love couples, too. I just didn't have much faith that my personal story would go that direction. At least that was one upside to this whole mess, I had a very good excuse for not immediately trying to get pregnant now that we were married.

We stood there and stared at each other for a long, long moment until Matt's radio crackled with a call for assistance. Matt responded that he was on his way and then looked at me. "I better get going."

"Yeah."

I bit my lip, trying not to cry or run to him. He didn't move, just stared at me for another long moment.

"Love you," he finally said.

"Love you, too."

"This'll be over soon. And then we can start that amazing life we have planned."

"Yeah."

I knew it was a lie. So did he. But I felt better for it.

Fancy and I didn't take our eyes off him until he got into his SUV and drove away. Only then did we go back inside and have ice cream. Lots and lots of ice cream.

CHAPTER 5

The next day was Easter. We didn't want to endanger anyone's health, but Sam was young and there are only so many Easter egg hunts a kid gets in a lifetime, you know? So we'd dyed boiled eggs the night before and then Trish and I had hid them along with a dozen plastic eggs in the wild area to the side of my grandpa's house.

Jack and Matt came, but they sat on the other side of the clearing. Trish had to continuously remind Sam to keep his distance. It was heart-breaking.

I'd left Fancy locked up next door. It was her nap time and I didn't want to put her on the tether I'd have to use in the front yard of my grandpa's house since it didn't have a fence. For some reason she was fine on a leash, but put her on a tether and she forgot she was on it and would run to the end and get jerked backward.

While Trish helped Sam find the last few eggs my grandpa came over and stood next to me.

"Wouldn't it be nice if we could end all of this right now? Just open back up?"

"Of course it would, Grandpa. But unfortunately you can't intimidate a virus into doing what you want it to do. The only way to end this is to come up with a way to treat it or prevent it or to get people to stay away from each other long enough it stops transmitting. And, well, none of that's looking very promising right now."

He winked at me. "I have a plan."

"Grandpa." I turned to face him. "You think being stuck in your nice comfortable home with television and the ability to drive around when you want is bad, don't forget how much worse prison was. Not to mention those places are a nightmare right now. Do you really want to go back there?"

He just smiled. "Who's going to arrest me?"

"Matt. He wouldn't like it, but he'd do it."

"What's he going to charge me with?"

"I don't know yet. But I'm not liking the way your mind is going these days."

He took a long sip of his Coors and nodded towards where Sam had settled himself down on the grass to open each of the plastic eggs. Most had chocolate or other little candies, but the gold one had a twenty-dollar bill in it. I knew when he'd found it because his eyes went so wide they probably doubled in size and he ran around showing it to everyone.

Matt caught my eye and raised one eyebrow as Sam ran by, like, "Look isn't he cute. Don't you want one? I see you smiling over there." I just shook my head and laughed. Not the time, Matt. Not the time.

After the egg hunt we all settled into an appropriately distanced barbecue in the front yard with Matt and Jack at one table on the far side of the yard and Sam, Trish, my grandpa, and I at a table on the other side of the yard.

"How's Lesley?" I asked.

"Good. We've talked each night on the phone, but I didn't see her this week because she wanted to be able to spend the day with her grandkids. All of her kids and their families agreed to not go anywhere for the last week so they could safely be together."

"Good for them." I gave him a sidelong glance. "You know, I probably shouldn't be sitting so close to you given the fact that you've been sneaking off to hang out at Russell's house."

"Maggie May."

"Well it's true. You're being less safe than I am."

He didn't answer.

I tried to imagine what the next year of our lives was going to look like with us sniping at each other to see who was being safe enough and who was being too dangerous. And, really, how long could we expect a little kid like Sam to hang out at home?

This was a kid who'd ridden his bicycle through most of the valley to find me when his mom went missing. He wasn't the type to curl up in the corner with a good book. And there really are only so many fun TV shows or movies for kids.

After a while I had to image the fun of growing virtual radishes was going to wear off. (He was currently obsessed with some strange game that involved living on an island and growing radishes for animal creatures. He'd spent an hour trying to tell me about it and I still didn't get it. What happened to Pitfall? Or my personal childhood favorite, Happy Trails, which involved sliding little map squares around while your character tried to collect money bags and chase down the bad guy.)

(I know. Probably no one else on this planet played that game. But I had an old Intellivision game console that my dad gave me and I'd play it for hours until my thumbs developed blisters from the tiny little buttons on the controller. Now games were about, I don't know, building things? Growing things? Character development? It was weird. It confused me. I just liked games I could win. Puzzles I could solve. Where there was one answer.)

I looked around at our sad little family gathering. No Abe and Evan. No Greta. No Jamie and Mason. No friends of Sam's. Of course I wanted it over. I don't like feeling powerless.

But we'd make it through. All of us. Alive.

Because that much I could control. I couldn't change the fact that this thing existed. I couldn't change the fact that it had spread the way it had. I couldn't make some stranger stay home or wash their hands or keep their distance or make safe choices.

But I could do that for myself. And I could guilt the hell out of everyone around me until they did, too.

And if that failed…

Well, I wasn't above a little sabotage to protect those I loved. What's an alternator cable between friends, right?

CHAPTER 6

I tried to keep a better eye on my grandpa the next couple of days. He was supposed to be staying away from Lesley still since they'd both been potentially exposed at their respective parties, but he kept leaving the house anyway. The third day in a row he did it, I decided to use my spare key and sneak into his house to see what I could find out.

I know. I'm a horrible person. We have established this fact. It should not be new to you or anyone else.

And normally I would not break into anyone's home, let alone the home of someone I love and who should be able to trust me. But I knew he was up to something and I also knew that whatever it was was the type of thing that was going to land him in jail.

And since I loved my grandpa and didn't want to see that happen, I needed to know what was going on. So my options were follow him to wherever he was going, which was likely Russell's house, which would do me no good, or break into his house and see if he'd left any notes around anywhere.

It wasn't a proud moment. But it was a necessary one.

A Housebound Holiday

What I found printed out neatly on his kitchen table didn't make a lot of sense to me.

First, he'd printed out the rates page for the Homesteader's Haven, a luxury camping retreat on the edge of Bakerstown. The place had replica teepee and covered wagons that people could sleep in that were nicer than a four-star hotel room. It was like extreme glamping. The beds in each one were king-sized, there was cable TV, and A/C in the summer, which was, quite frankly, more than any of us locals had.

The only accommodation people had to make when they stayed there was that the restrooms and dining/cooking area were communal.

My grandpa had circled the rates and made a couple calculations in the margins for what it would cost for someone to stay for fourteen days straight. There were also some notes to the side that made it look like he'd called the place and asked what a long-term rate would be for staying there.

I flipped through the stack and saw that he'd done the same for a handful of other properties in the area, including the Creek Inn, which my friends Abe and Evan ran.

That gave me an idea and I called Abe to ask him about it, but he said he really didn't know what my grandpa was up to. Just that he'd wanted their long-term rate and some idea about their capacity.

"How are you guys doing?" I asked, knowing they had to be struggling with the shutdown of their business.

"We were lucky. We don't need to be open. We own the place outright, so we've just been enjoying some time off. Neither one of us want to take the risk of getting sick."

"And your staff?"

"Well, luckily, this is our slow time of the year, so we just kept the few year-round staff on payroll. Managed to get one of those loans so it won't even cost us anything for a couple months."

"Oh, that's good. How's Lucy Carrots holding up?" (That was their St. Bernard who was absolutely adorable.)

"She misses the guests. They spoiled her rotten. But I think she's enjoying having us around more. How's Fancy?"

"Did I mention that Trish and Sam are living with us right now?"

"Oh."

"Yes. Oh." I glanced out the window. "You know, I better get going. I'm standing in my grandpa's kitchen without his permission, and if he comes home and finds me it may not go over well."

"Maggie! You broke into your grandpa's house?"

"It's not really breaking in if you have a key is it?"

His silence told me what he thought of that one.

"Anyway. Better go. Glad you're doing well. Bye."

"Bye."

I glanced at the other papers in the stack, but they were just as confusing as the rest of them. Something about freezer trucks and their capacity and how they worked.

As I let myself back out the front door I knew my grandpa was up to something, but what it was exactly I still wasn't sure. Maybe making everyone who entered the valley quarantine for fourteen days? That certainly made a lot of sense, but I couldn't see it actually working.

Look at that family in Chicago who'd exposed a whole school because they wanted to go to a Daddy-daughter dance. I mean, seriously. People are…

Selfish. We'll go with selfish. Or perhaps, not self-aware? I don't know. Whatever they are, you can't rely on them to "do the right thing" on their own most of the time.

As I closed the front door and walked back to my house, I wondered what my grandpa was up to. It had to be more than just researching quarantine options.

CHAPTER 7

I grabbed Fancy and took her up to the big rock behind my grandpa's house. As she ate a doggie ice cream, I called Jamie to see how she was doing and to run everything by her. Maybe she could see something I couldn't.

"Maggie! How are you holding up?"

"You sound far too happy given the current circumstances. Can I offer you an eight-year-old child and his mother as house guests for the next year or so?"

She laughed. "Not going so well, huh?"

"I am not equipped for this. I should be hiding out somewhere with just me and Fancy. And *maybe* Matt. On a good day."

She laughed again.

"Seriously, why are you so happy? You're stuck at home, too."

"I know. But…"

I had a sudden suspicion I didn't want to hear what came next.

"But?"

"Well, we weren't going to tell anyone until we hit the three-month mark, but we're almost there, and…"

A Housebound Holiday

"You're pregnant?"

"I am! Isn't it great? Oh, I'm so excited. I've been looking at all these decoration ideas for the baby's room. I know you'd probably want to do something crazy like a zig-zag black and white border and red or something, but I think we're going to go with yellow and green pastel. And giraffes. Or elephants. Or maybe teddy bears. Or maybe all three. I don't know. There are so many choices. And with the lockdown happening, I've just thrown myself into it. I'm also doing a ton of research on baby foods. I see no reason I can't make my own."

I laughed. That was the one part of the conversation I could grab hold of. "From what I hear, you're going to be pretty darned tired those first few months. So maybe don't try to add making your own baby food on top of it."

"Yeah, you're probably right. But I'm still going to research it all and try different types anyway even if I don't make them for my own kid. Maybe I can start a baby food company up and have it running by the time the second one comes along. And then I can just grab a few jars out of the storage room when I need them. If not by the second, then certainly by the third."

"Exactly how many kids are you planning on having?"

I figured maybe you should have one and see how it goes before you start thinking you like it enough to add more into the mix.

"I don't know. At least three? Maybe more?"

I opened my mouth to mention to her that sometimes that wasn't possible. And that sometimes people change their mind after the first one or, most definitely, after the second one.

But then I closed it again.

This was a moment of joy in an otherwise bleak year and I was not going to ruin it with my realism. "I am so happy for you, Jamie."

"Thank you. I was so worried about getting pregnant, but here we are. And, I know the world is crazy right now and maybe if we'd waited a couple more months we would've put it off, but I'm so glad we didn't."

"I'll have to throw you a baby shower. Maybe a virtual one, given the circumstances."

"We'll have to Zoom once my belly gets big enough so you can see it."

"Absolutely." I wanted to cry. Because life was changing so fast. In good ways. But, scary ways. To hide it from Jamie, I changed the subject. "Speaking of…"

I told her about my grandpa and the strange conversation we'd had and what I'd found on his kitchen table and how worried I was that he was about to do something drastic.

After lecturing me about how I shouldn't have broken into his house, Jamie said, "I wonder what his plan is? I hope he can pull it off, whatever it is."

"Jamie!"

"I do. I want my best friend here for my pregnancy. And I want to be able to leave my house without worrying about catching this thing. Can you imagine?"

I shuddered, thinking of the few stories that had made the news about pregnant women whose kids had been born while they were in comas or who had kids that needed to be kept in the NICU that they couldn't see for more than an hour or two a day. I didn't want that for my best friend.

Heck. I didn't want that for my worst enemy.

"Yeah. I just…I don't want my grandpa to go to prison, Jamie."

"If he pulls this off, whatever it is, no one is going to put him in prison."

"Not even Officer Clark?" (Who had hated my grandpa forever and still probably thought he'd killed Jack Dunner despite all evidence to the contrary.)

"He has a newborn. You imagine he doesn't go to work every day scared about catching this? He's been staying at his cousin's to keep his wife and baby safe."

"Oh. I didn't know that."

"Yeah. So, no, I don't think even Officer Clark will arrest him. It's people outside the valley that are going to be the problem, not people in the valley. But if we don't let them in then they can't do anything about it, right? Pretty much everyone I know would be grateful for a way to get on with our lives already."

"But what about tourism? So many people depend on it to live. This may last a year or more. People have bills to pay."

"I'll put Mason on it."

"What do you mean?"

"His family has enough money. If they can't help people through this, then I'll divorce his sorry you-know-what. He can make loans if he really feels that's required, but I'd rather see him just help people out. That's what a community does, isn't it? We come together when we're needed? I mean, really. Debt is just so much paper. This is about lives."

"That may be what a community should do. But, well, look at the world. We don't do that for each other on a normal basis. Why would anyone start now?"

"Because it's the right thing to do. And this isn't the world. This is the Baker Valley. We can make it work here."

"Hm. If you think so…"

"I do. You should call Greta. And I'm going to go corner Mason before baby brain makes me forget."

"Do you already have baby brain?"

"I don't know. Probably not. I probably just have information overload from doomscrolling day in and day out. I'd rather focus on this instead. Make the world a better place, one valley at a time, right? Talk to you later. Bye."

"Bye."

As I stared down at my grandpa's house, I tried to figure out how I'd managed to *add* members to my grandpa's conspiracy rather than defuse the whole situation. But Jamie did have a good point. If we could all pull together and agree to get through this, we should be able to make it work.

And if Mason Maxwell put his family's money and clout behind whatever hare-brained scheme my grandpa was cooking up that made it far less likely he'd be arrested. And far more likely he could actually pull off the plan, whatever it turned out to be.

CHAPTER 8

So I called Greta. (Thanks to good marriage choices she had a few hundred million dollars to work with and she'd come from humble enough beginnings that she might actually be willing to do it, too.)

"Maggie, so good to hear from you," she said when she answered the phone, her German accent as present as ever.

"Greta. How are you holding up?"

"Well, it was sad to have to cancel my visit to see Jean-Philippe in Paris, but otherwise, I am good. I have taken up jewelry making."

"Really?"

"Oh yes. It is a very soothing hobby."

"What kind of jewelry?"

"All kinds. I have worked with nail polishes and necklace bases to create pretty swirled patterns. And I have worked with wire and beads and jewels. I will send you something. Or I will give you something next time I see you. If I ever get to see you again. We are not doing so well here, Maggie. This country…I love it, but…I do not understand."

"Oh trust me, neither do most of us. No matter what side of the divide we're on. Speaking of…If we turn the Baker Valley into an isolated enclave until all this passes, any chance you'd be willing to help the residents out so they don't all end up bankrupt at the end? Maybe make some loans that don't have to be paid back immediately to get them through?"

"An isolated enclave? Explain."

"I may have accidentally given my grandpa the idea that if he could somehow keep people from coming to the valley that he could go back to living his normal life in a couple weeks. I was going to try to stop him, but Jamie thinks it's a good idea and maybe she's right. Problem is, how do people make a living until then? Or, if not make a living, meet their obligations at least. I mean, honestly, a roof over your head and food on your table should be all we're worried about, but people have mortgage payments and credit card payments and car payments and, well, debt, you know? It doesn't go away."

"Ah, yes, I see. This is a challenge. Because the people are here, but the debt is not."

"Right. I wish we could just pause everything for a couple weeks—just all stay in place, no one owes anyone anything for that period of time and then it would be over. But that won't happen."

"Hm, yes. American priorities. How many people are we talking?"

"About fifteen thousand or so." (That was the population of the county at least. I'd looked it up on my phone before I called her.) "Some will have savings to get through with. Some will have businesses that can still run. Some won't have debt. But that's how many we'd have to help if we manage this."

(When had *I* joined the conspiracy? Sometime between sitting down on a rock above a small Colorado town and now it seemed.)

"And how long would we need to plan for?"

"Maybe a year?"

"Give me a moment." I heard the sound of her fingernails clicking on keys and the whir of an adding machine crunching numbers. Finally, she made a small harrumphing sound. "I think this would take two hundred million or so. It is not a small amount, but we can do this. Perhaps some loans for mortgages and other debt, but food we can just give. The question is, what is your grandpa's plan? Will it work?"

"Oh, and you won't be alone in doing this. Jamie is making Mason help, too."

"Good. Your grandpa's plan?"

"I don't know, to be honest."

"Hm. I will call him. We must make sure it is a good plan. I enjoy my jewelry-making but I would like to see you for coffee. And to have Hans and Fancy go to the park together. So we will do this. Even if your grandpa was not planning this, now I am. It will be good, Maggie. Goodbye."

She hung up on me and I wondered what exactly I'd started. Even if I had no further involvement in the matter, between the conversations I'd had with my grandpa, Jamie, and Greta, I had definitely been the one to spur things along from "wouldn't it be nice" to something that was actually going to happen.

I considered calling Matt to let him know about everything, but Fancy decided she'd had enough of hanging out on a rock and started pulling at her leash to please be walked.

🐾🐾 42 🐾🐾

CHAPTER 9

It was two in the morning a few days later when I heard a loud rumbling noise like the canyon outside of town was collapsing. Knowing what I knew about my grandpa's friendships with people who knew how to use explosives, I immediately jumped out of bed and threw on a sweatshirt and some shoes.

(The nice thing about sleeping in the type of pajamas that can be seen by your neighbors without causing a scandal is that you can be dressed and out the door in a minute or so if need be. A habit I'd acquired when Fancy was a puppy who needed to be walked immediately or else.)

It was only one block down to the highway and two blocks to the beginning of the canyon, so I didn't bother with my van, just walked briskly. I took Fancy with me since she wouldn't stop barking. She does *not* like to be woken from a deep sleep, thank you very much.

I couldn't see any signs of a rock slide, but what I did find were a series of large concrete construction barriers placed across the highway so that there was no access to the canyon, and my grandpa and Officer Clark looking smug and talking quietly as they leaned side-by-side against the barrier.

"Gentlemen," I said.

My grandpa stood up. "Maggie May. Figured you'd be out here as soon as you heard it."

"And what exactly did I hear, Grandpa?"

"Well, don't you just know that there are some horrible rockslides in Colorado? Shut the whole highway down sometimes. And it turns out we just had one ourselves. A big one. The type that will shut down the canyon for…gosh, I don't know. Months?"

"Did we?"

He nodded, a slight smile quirking his lips.

"And let me guess, the highway outside of Bakerstown had the same issue? Same night even? Such a strange coincidence."

"That it did. Or so Officer Clark here tells me. Tragic all those strangers won't be able to come here for Memorial Day or the Fourth."

"And if I was wrong about this thing? If it clears up faster than I think it will?"

"Well, wouldn't you know it? There might be some construction equipment that unexpectedly frees itself up and we can get things fixed much sooner. But for now, we're just gonna have to live here together and make it work. Good thing your friend Greta brought in a nice big helicopter for emergencies. And that Mason Maxwell arranged for all sorts of extra food to be stored on his property before all this happened. And, of course, I imagine the county council will put together some sort of financial assistance for all those who are impacted financially by this so no one suffers."

"What if someone doesn't like this?"

He shrugged. "Nice thing about those helicopters is they can fly someone right on out of here. But they won't be allowed to fly them back."

I shook my head in defeat. "You did good, Grandpa. But what about Evan and Abe? I assume they're stuck on the other side of that rock slide of yours?"

"Wouldn't you know it? They decided to stay at the Homesteader's Haven for a few nights so they were already in the valley when it happened. And it turns out Greta has a nice little furnished property she normally rents out that's just going to be sitting there vacant now that I'd bet they can stay in until this all passes."

"What if we're just locking the illness in with us, though?"

"Speaking of that, I heard the council is going to impose a lockdown starting at midnight tomorrow. One of those serious, European-type lockdowns where no one goes anywhere for two weeks. Someone needs food, they'll drop it off for them. Only exception are cops, fire, and doctors or nurses willing to stay at the hospital. Or so I hear."

"You thought of everything."

"Me? Oh no. You thought of everything, my dear. We just made it work." He winked at me as he walked over and put his arm around my shoulder. "Now. It's the middle of the night. How about we walk back home and let Officer Clark handle this 'til morning?"

EPILOGUE

Once people understood that they'd be taken care of through however long this mess lasted most were happy to have the valley walled off from the rest of the world for a while if it meant getting back to some sense of normalcy.

Greta flew the few remaining dissidents out of the valley and gave them a nice generous payment to settle in elsewhere until things cleared up. It helped that the council made it very clear that you either went along with the new plan or left.

I still figured it wasn't going to be quite as easy as it looked right now, because there would definitely be those who did not agree with what had been done, but I still had hope it would be better than the alternative.

And I was glad to know that I lived in a place where people were willing to make those sacrifices for one another. Mason and Greta could've bunkered down secure in their mansions and let the rest of the valley suffer, but they hadn't. And they weren't the only ones who'd agreed to help out. The county council had set up a donation fund and over 2,500 people had contributed in the first two weeks.

We were committed to helping one another through this. It felt good.

But what was even better was when Matt was finally able to come home two weeks later.

I was so excited I literally jumped on him as soon as he walked through the door even though I wasn't sure he was going to be able to catch me. I didn't care if we fell to the floor in a heap, at least we'd be doing it together.

After he finished kissing me hello he asked, "Where's Fancy?"

"At my grandpa's for the night. I know she's missed you and I know you've missed her, but I wanted twenty-four hours alone with my husband where all I have to think about is you and how wonderful it is that we can finally be together in this blessedly-silent home."

"All alone?"

I nodded.

"All alone."

"Then let's not waste a moment." He picked me up and carried me to our room.

(And the rest of that twenty-four hours? Well, that's none of your business now, is it?)

🐾 🐾 🐾

*For the next Maggie May and Miss Fancypants Mystery, check out **A Fouled-Up Fourth**.*

ABOUT THE AUTHOR

When Aleksa Baxter decided to write what she loves it was a no-brainer to write a cozy mystery set in the mountains of Colorado where she grew up and starring a Newfie, Miss Fancypants, that is very much like her own Newfie, in both the good ways and the bad.

You can reach her at aleksabaxterwriter@gmail.com or on her website aleksabaxter.com.